# FRUMA

*Caught in Her Web*

# FRUMA

*Caught in Her Web*

Dr. David Rabeeya

Copyright © 2006 by Dr. David Rabeeya.

Library of Congress Number:     2006900383
ISBN:          Softcover        1-4257-0724-6

All rights reserved. No part of this book may be reproduced or transmitted in any form or by any means, electronic or mechanical, including photocopying, recording, or by any information storage and retrieval system, without permission in writing from the copyright owner.

This is a work of fiction. Names, characters, places and incidents either are the product of the author's imagination or are used fictitiously, and any resemblance to any actual persons, living or dead, events, or locales is entirely coincidental.

This book was printed in the United States of America.

To order additional copies of this book, contact:
Xlibris Corporation
1-888-795-4274
www.Xlibris.com
Orders@Xlibris.com
32905

To Arlene with love and thanks.
Dedicated to Arlene Shenkus for her continuous
support in our struggle to find meaning beyond
words and actions.

# Acknowledgement

I wish to thank Arlene Shenkus for her editorial work in the preparation of this novel for publication. Her incredible dedication to the struggles and victories of women has deeply touched my heart. This has taught me strength, spirituality and faith. In addition I wish to recognize Mr. Brockton Youngman for his efforts in the typing of this manuscript.

# Chapter 1

It happened in the market of humanity. Her walk was a walk of young women that life has decided all things for her. She was bent and wrapped up with flowery fabric, which constantly clashed with her surroundings. Her hair is hidden under a brown handkerchief, which urgently needed a fine wash. She came to shop in one of many Jewish delicatessens along her New York Street. She was a shadow walking in the direction of the sun, knowing that it is a futile journey. She was already about thirty but her marriage was consummated at the age of seventeen. Her large family consisted of nine girls and her father was walking angry with God. He did not have someone to say Kaddish after his death. A curse he thought not to have a male baby. Her mother had already aged beyond recognition. In a haredi family women are recognized by their frailty and domestic skills. Her father was always walking murmuring fragmented words in Yiddish and

Hebrew. She is young with five children. She is pregnant again because God wanted her to be this way.

Most women in her neighborhood looked alike, long dresses and long sleeves, long days and nights and short memories. She could not allow herself to remember the past. The present was always knocking on her door with her not knowing what her abstract future will bring. Couplets of her red hair were showering from under her "shumata" scarf but her penetrating blue eyes were surrendering her physical beauty. Even under heavy cloth real men could easily notice her delicate heaving breathing breasts and her twisted, gentle behind. While layers upon layers were stuffed under her dress it was not easy to ignore her delicate feminine movement leaving hidden desire for those men who allow themselves to imagine women. Her black shoes and long socks have imprisoned her long legs. Her lips were more than red, wide and awesome in their length and width shouting for fiery desire in the market of routine. Those lips did not possess lipstick, but many men can only envy her man in their secretive heart. She was like a sexual creature covered with plenty of religious customs and more denying the artistic world of the divine.

Sometimes she inclined to pick up the fresh tomatoes from the baskets. Her custom was to squeeze some of the tomatoes until she wet her hands with the greenish, yellowish juice. She always licked the seeds like a hungry cat. She always apologized and bought the red fruit. It looks like her face was turning red; embarrassment had married enjoyment. Something about squeezing tomatoes activated the juices in her body. Wetness, together with ticklish feelings, has dominated her again and again. When these events occurred she instinctively read fragmented verses from *Tzena Wurena* to calm herself. It was not like the moments in which her husband blessed the lord before he knows her biblically. She was always stoned in these moments of divine knowledge. She once heard about orgasm and she couldn't fathom why women need it since the idea is to please Hashem because children are the only blessing in sex. She feared her God of the patriarch and matriarch. He was her source of vengeance and mercy. She prayed to him many times with such adherence that her breath was taken away. She also fainted because she loved her Adonay so much. She learned the art of submission to all male categories: her God, her husband, and his organ. She could not believe that her satisfaction was translated into tomato squeezing as well as her very personal deity. Her husband was eating tomato salad for years now, curious but not inquisitive. She always collected the seeds from his plate and ate them with great appetite near him. He used to smile to this frenzy for tomato seeds but she was obedient in many other areas and he forgave her for this unusual habit.

Fruma, she was called. Her name compelled her to form an image of righteousness, a pure and kosher character before a community of those who fear God and women. Many in the haredi community always said, "Fruma is a woman of valor, Fruma is like Sara our first mother. Fruma is an excellent wife for her husband and children. No wonder they call her Fruma. After all her name means clean, pure, and innocent." She worked as a seamstress in her time, sowing, fixing, repairing and consulting other women were her various jobs. Taking care of their daughters was extra. She was constantly tired and exhausted. However, she always had time to listen attentively to her husband. He had complaints about his mild rabbinic teachings in the yeshiva. He always sweated in his armpits and his brown busy beard and in the heat of the summer and in the cold of winter he wore the same black and white uniform. The hat was in the standard department. The hat is large in size with the huge black yarmulka removed constantly by his nervous hands. He studied his Talmud's pages and taught to others who dressed like him. Meager income and plenty of aggravation and frustration were his sacrifice to his God on earth. A teacher and a seamstress Fruma thought... But God can always supply sustenance. Being humble and poor is apparently a fine omen for her destiny.

Reb Paltiel, his family called him. Palti, his disciples called him. Palti was always in a hurry to meet his God in prayer after prayer. Swinging, moving and shaking with closed eyes he prayed. He wished to be spiritual and busy thus avoiding everyday life. It was safe, convenient and quite comfortable. Fruma was somehow in the background because the Jewish law was always calling him to place him before his wife and his daughters. He did not know how to deal with girl's stuff. Monthly bloody cycles, brassiness, itching vagina and inflammation are for his wife and daughters. They are aliens from different planets. In the yeshiva he met frustrated, horny teenage students since women were nothing but a fantasy of the evil impulse and even Satan himself to boys of this age. It was easy for him to tell his male students to fight their sexual instincts. Burning themselves in the holy texts with intensive legal arguments was his principle cure. Fruma had told him in the dark nights about rumors. Rumors like yeshiva "buchurs" seeking the service of harlots in some dark allies of the Big Apple. He brushed aside these rumors, always blaming the secular Jews who try to plant embarrassment and shame in his community. Fruma nodded in agreement while her small voice was telling her that what she is witnessing is only traces of asteroids, which struck established religion from the time of God's conception. Fruma talked to herself without stopping. Often she talked to herself in her dreams. She normally remained silent in intercourse. Palti does not hug and whisper words, exciting words of the illusive romantic love. He just fulfilled his duty and in his heart he was satisfying Adoshem which is far more superior to Fruma's interest.

Guilt, anger, frustration and despair were always prominent in her fantastic dreams after she peeked at the poster of semi naked men and women on the bus to the train station. At the same time she felt that she should not be in that bus. It is unusual for her to be with "goyim" and secular Jews. Definitely she should not be sitting near them. They will only see her as alien in the masses in New York. Smelling the body odors of men with traces of after shave was alien to her. Seeing brown, white and black young teenage girls, their shorts in the size of a tie was unnerving. Their brassieres revealed about two thirds of their sound bosoms. They are giggling and talking nonsense as if life concentrated on their sole activities. Men of all ages are looking at these girls and women with drooling saliva unable to express their real thoughts. Restricted by legalism and cultural mores, they remain silent. Fruma is conversing with herself again. This is Sodom and Gomorra, she contemplated. This is total freedom and anarchy. Liberty and chaos, she concluded. She is convinced that someone is following her, the feeling that she is committing a crime on this journey on a routine bus. Men in her view were like "shmata." Silent, quiet and worried. About what? No clue!

She does not have any reason or excuse to be far away from her synagogue before erev Rosh-Hashana. Some people were staring at her, but it is an empty look by millions in this metropolis without any connections to themselves and others. She felt like just a digit in a boring PhD dissertation about abstract statistical data. A couple was kissing. She can see how the man is aroused. His tight jeans surrendered the movements in their center. She rushed to her well-wrapped sandwich. A ripe tomato was calling her, eager to be consumed by her burning lips. Slowly she began pushing the fruit in her delicate mouth, enjoying every bite. Some seeds had fallen on her dress and the yellow stains became noticeable to the naked eye. Can the God of her neighborhood see her in her desert journey on a slow bus going somewhere between the skyscrapers? What is the meaning of getting up before sunset? Having to pray and make blessings over anything and everything. Helping her daughters in chores before their departure to their all girls' religious school? She has also to feed Paltiel with his incredible appetite. Yesterdays were dedicated to cooking and cooking again with other women who were gossiping, but with profound guilt about this offense against God who loves Yiddish more than Hebrew. She had completed several years of religious studies when they matched her with Rev. Paltiel. The might of the loss of her virginity was an uneventful occurrence. She was dazed somehow during this speedy act. Palti blessed his beloved God and scattered his seeds all over her inner flesh.

She was fascinated by the jeans, which were worn by almost everyone in this endless trip on her anonymous bus. Unconsciously she touched her thighs imagining one blue pair embracing them. She blocked and an electric wave went gently through her spine. She began noticing a noticeable enlargement in her breast, sweating heavily without control. It seemed that the plastic in her underwear had shrunk, leaving her besieged by usual pressures on her body and soul. She began talking to the matriarchs in Yiddish. She especially loved Rachel. She was a tragic figure. Loved by Jacob. Losing her life in her birth of Benjamin. Her grave was not places with other matriarchs and patriarchs. She was buried near Bethlehem. Alone. She was buried outside the main road. Rachel always comforted her, telling her that troubles can purify humans if she can take it. She can take it. She told her that God would not offer troubles to those who cannot handle them. Fruma knew that things do not work this way but it was soothing to echo Rachel's faith in women's future victories. Promises received from her God about reward to the righteous and punishment to evil was not working recently. Rachel was not able to supply satisfying answers to this dilemma of a haredi woman. Palti always gently strokes his beard to accentuate his process of thinking. At least he thought that this movement of the hand on the facial hair could produce for men pearls of wisdom.

The driver, huge and black, was looking at Fruma through the front mirror mesmerized by her sealed body, unable to see anything but a huge bag of humanity sitting at the back of the bus traveling endlessly from the first station to the terminal in order to repeat the same cycle. He did not even bother her. He did not ask for new fees. Homeless woman, he thought. Let her be protected from the wintry rain and the needles of the cold. Fruma has so many things to observe in this trip around New York in one day, as if her family is not in existence, as if her God had told her to go in circles until she neglects any responsibility. If God will punish her for her moving adventure, how can she satisfy him? This powerful God who can see and hear everything! This is the same God who can also guess our inclinations and thoughts before we trigger our brain and before we say a syllable or even a letter. Just how? Maybe! Just maybe! The entire issue of God is one huge human conspiracy to control us? Maybe everything is a fluke? But Palti said that was the way of the pagans. Jews must believe that Hashem is conducting everything, if we like it or not. Fruma thought again: "If my function in this world is to offer my vagina for the sake of new Jewish children and to obey the male species—why am I here? Servant to everyone . . . but they call me a queen in my haredi congregation. What kind of a queen am I if I do not have subjects?"

It seems that the Rabbis of the past were hypocrites after all. They would praise weddings, marriages and children but they never wish to hear the sounds of words from women. She feels like the wheels of the bus. Without wheels nothing can move, but the motor is the man in this invention. Wheels get dirty. They attract dirt, human waste, and gravel and they always go in predicted cycles. To her astonishment the driver just out of nowhere grabbed a juicy tomato and ate it with such a great appetite, splashing seeds on his uniform. The tomato, she thought, is considered to be a vegetable by many, but it is a fruit. You can eat it just like that—you can preclude juice and catch all from it. You can use it as blood in fake movies when people are supposed to be injured. You can place it with pasta. You can dry it. You can use it like cucumbers in salt and vinegar. You can play with its seeds and plant new tomatoes. It is green before it becomes red. "Tomato is my favorite fruit," Fruma murmured quietly. "However, it has so many functions," she smiled as if she does not believe herself when she monologued. "Maybe cucumber is stronger, but they are all water. They enter the body and in minutes they lose their effectiveness." She blushed for a couple of seconds, but allegory excited her. Last time she was in a bus was with haredi women on their way to summer camp in the Catskills. Baskets of chicken, meat and fish dispersed a heavy aroma of women who took pride in their cooking.

She spoke about the achievements of her daughters and about their future husbands. They need to learn about Jewish men who will study "Halacha" and spend their lives arguing about past religious arguments. She needed men with prestige: fearing God and studying non-stop from Humash's texts. Fruma had established her priorities like her engagement and marriage. Her five daughters deserved pious men who trust God and learn and learn without end religious text in its written and oral forms. She was dreaming about being a grandma at the age of forty-five. Maybe even a great grandmother at the age of fifty-six. Her daughter will produce at least ten nice Jewish children. All of them will be scholars of Talmud. They will all wear side locks demonstrating symbolically their literal adherence to the" midrashic" interpretations of the divine verse. They will all wear Talit Katan and pray and pray with devotion and love of the God of Israel who loves his people, but often has left them hanging in the air. After a while she noticed that a man with brown skin and burning brown eyes was staring at her for a long time. He looks like an Arab and his look has scared her hellish earth. He was reading a newspaper in a language other than Hebrew, Yiddish and English. New people entered the bus and others left it, but the commotion and the noise continued to dominate many conversations about human trivial concerns. This time she paid attention to examples of hairstyles and colors, earrings, decorative jewelry and tattoos up and down the bodies. Some men were wearing rainbows of silver and gold chains on their necks and legs showing the world their concept of secular fashion. From reason she needed to say the "Shma." She was wondering why now? All of a sudden she was shaking like a leaf in the wind of the fall. Fear from her fate in the next world always occupied a great deal of her time and efforts. She had imagination. Can God teach women in paradise? Can she relive after her death, after the arrival of the Jewish messiah?

She is willing to return immediately to her safe and violent haredi neighborhood. At least they fight there about the letter of the holy text but here in the hedonic bus people kill each other for a couple of dollars if an opportunity delivers itself. In a flashback Fruma remembered the drunken Hasidic Jews, the thieves, the wife beaters hand all of them were wearing the holy vest and the huge round hats. They were cheating and praying. Not all of them, but some of them. And them, she watched them contributing "tzedaka" to the poor. These contradictions have eaten away at her slowly. Doubts came and went, but it is also a fact that her mother has accused her in her childhood with questionable belief in the male powerful Shadday. This was just one episode, which was forgotten and appeared again in this unique bus. She wanted to study in the college for female teachers and to teach Torah but her marriage has placed her chest in the front of life at the expense of her brain. Her babies sucked her nipples powerfully. She loved those intimate days because she adored the state of motherhood. But! They have depleted her, these hungry and smelly babies. Slowly but surely she began walking as a zombie between sleep deprivation and shitty diapers. Paltiel just snored through it all. He was giving his energy to the books of the invisible God. Fruma was investing herself in everyone but herself. And some of these haredi

Jews, they fight over nonsense; the number of drops in the Mikvah, the level of the glut kosher, the kosher ingredients of Passover's toothpaste, the wigs of their women and their ingredients, the genius of their provincial rabbi, the ultimate halachic correctness based on their rabbis' supposed knowledge of the will of God, the hysterical admiration of their rev. There were also fights over the remains of his food on his plate, the instructions about their business, mates, housing and jobs.

Fruma opened the windows near her to breathe the cold wind in a city, which is turning white because Christmas was approaching soon. Almost everyone was nice to each other for a couple of days and then again man to man as wolf. The music about salvation, peace and harmony almost brought her to strangulation of people near the golden calf. She could not stand anymore the artificial plastic humanity in the grayish surrounding. Many haredim do the same, she thought. This is complex with regard to other Jews and intolerance toward Reform Jews and non-Ashkenazic Jews. Fruma saw the ghettoes of the Ukraine, Poland and Russia in her religious streets. Isolated proud and rejectionist. Fearing the universal because it threatens their particulars. Spending wasted times or wasted subjects. Fruma was almost in a state of self-hatred when she noticed the dark shadow over the lost city covering crimes and brutality with shiny neon lights and colorful bulbs.

# Chapter 2

The police were in her house since Palti was scared to death in her absence. Devastated after her disappearance, he contacted everyone with any influence. Rumors are the flood which nourish the unknowing, especially in those who adopted ghetto life. It seems that more imaginative energy is invested in the haredi congregation. Because everyone knew about Fruma and Fruma knew a great deal about other women, Fruma heard later that she was kidnapped, killed, raped, and eloped to Mexico because she ran away with a lover. There are those who even spread rumors about her loss of mental stability. The shouts of Palti and the tears of her daughters together with the gathering of hundreds welcomed her near her humble home. Someone even volunteered to ask the chief rev to come and bless her in the presence of her family and friends in order to remove any evil eye, which has struck her unconsciously. Many run to the shul to pray prayers of thanksgiving about her safe return. Fruma never understood all this commotion about a ride on the bus, several tomatoes and one journey in a city of millions. Palti demands answers and Fruma, exhausted and hungry, begs him to delay the report to the early dawn of morning. Palti, with his injured ego and with the burden of public embarrassment and shame, could not nudge. Fruma told him about a bus without stops, but Palti was left puzzled with suspicions. He convinced himself that only demons could cause a haredi woman to wander far away from her home. She could not convince him that she could not leave her bus because the bus had wheels and wheels can only return to their first position to start the round trip again. The more she talks about the bus and wheels, the more livid he becomes. He thanks the policemen about their search and he locked himself in a room with Fruma. Their daughters just place their ears on the wall, but only defining silence was heard. Palti was whispering words about love, dignity, the avenging God and the irresponsibility of abandonment. Fruma was sobbing quietly, unable to utter a word. Suddenly the light was turned off and darkness and silence have taken over their time and space.

As if she went through a nightmare episode, Fruma woke up rushing to her domestic routine, secluded, and walking gently like a cat in an ambush. Her words were few, but her body was sending messages of pain and aches. The female doctor in the neighborhood area has prescribed some pills to relax her soul, but Fruma gently threw them in the bathroom's water. The rabbitzen came to comfort her and bless her with ancient kabbalistic blessings. Fruma was polite and thankful, but in her heart she felt the void of an empty tomato. Her husband was suspicious that her unusual consumption of tomatoes was a fine sign of pregnancy. However, Fruma had assured him that her moods are her moods and her conception was not in existence. She was refusing to leave home for weeks now. She placed her energy in sewing and repairing clothes of others. She tried reading the local haredi "haness." Nothing interested her in the publication. She was bored with religion. The announced conferences and demonstrations, hacks against reform, conservative and Reconstructionist Jews and eloquent curses against Israel, which was called the "Zionist entity" by the editor. Boring! Dry! Repetition! Praises to this rev and that rev! Who cares? Real and unreal fear from the "schvartze," a derogatory term to describe blacks. Snow began falling and the temperature outside has chased even dogs away. This was the time to stay between the walls and pay high bills to heat the houses. In the small talk of haredi men and women many decided that the changing behavior of Fruma derived from the dibbuk that stick to her soul not enabling her to explain a missing day in her life and her hiding within her walls. The "dibbek" is some kind of evil forces, which can penetrate the body of those who are struck by it. Some believe that there is a need for a special ceremonial process to extract the evil spirit. Fruma just smiled in her heart about all these superstitious mythological beliefs she knew. She is normal in her book. The bus and the wheels have shaken her to her roots, but she is more pensive and reflective now. Some form of metamorphosis occurred in her through.

This is a change, which cannot be explained. All that she needs is to speak with someone that she can trust. Just to vent her frustration with a new unexplained state of mind. Secular Jews used psychiatrists to talk to and radical changes in their life made this necessary. They're not crazy. They are either lonely middle class Jews who are looking for meaning or they are those who hope that dashing out with the garbage will facilitate their transition to some tranquility in the heart. The blessings of the chief rev were nice. The care of female friends was appreciated, but she lied about her six pregnancies and Paltiel went berserk. She lied about several things and lying is not allowed in the commandments. However, many lies can sometimes delay the crisis. She was hoping against hope that somehow the issue will be reduced. It is never resolved. She knew it. But she is caught between the interpretation of her religion by men and her particular female context. As a matter of fact, she had already lied on her daily prayers and she denied her natural intelligence to think for herself outside their powerful partners. Her Jewish God and her Jewish husbands.

One day without warning in a fateful circumstance without logic she turned day and she saw the brown guy from the bus walking in her neighborhood wearing a yarmulke with an Israeli newspaper. He did not recognize her. She could swear that this was the Mediterranean gentleman in her bus. She never imagined that some Jews can be religiously Jewish and culturally an Arab. She heard fragmented information about Jews in Arab and Muslim lands. These were Jews from a different planet. She knew that they are not familiar with Yiddish at all. The holocaust did not affect most of them. Sometimes they call them Sepharadim. Once she heard Paltiel telling her that they are not really Jews. They are primitive according to his perspective. He never met one of them but he knew. Fruma forgave her husband this time because she did not know about these strange creatures with brown skin that speak Arabic. He was walking to the house of the chief rabbi (the master rev) to find ways to cling to the mother religion after he experienced the beauty of secularism. Fruma was not sure if his name was Salman or Shlomo. Her neighbor was telling her about a sephardic Shabbatay Tzvi who came to find refuge under the wings of their Ashkenazi rev. Fruma learned that he is about forty-five. Born in Iraq, lived in Israel and migrated to America. A shrewd businessman who lost all his money because of bad investment and suddenly he found God. She is waging war against her macho God and this desperate man had begun to love God more than women. Fruma was an expert in the business of God. People usually love him slowly but found him quickly when they are called losers. He needed food, shelter and attention. He refused to be homeless and in their search he threw himself in the alien planet of Hasidic Jews. Iraq, Fruma thought, is at least many years of light from her community in Flatbush. The metamorphosis she noticed was fast. Salman began growing pious and someone donated the large hat with the long black jacket with white shirt under it. He looked like all the haredi. For, after all, they all look like Abe Lincoln, the Amish and penguins in March.

# Chapter 3

Fruma was curious by nature. Secretly she purchased a book and hid it under her undershirt and underwear. Who is this salesman? It is very easy to recognize him; he looks like an Arab. His accent is so Semitic, whatever the meaning of this statement! Married? Children? Family far away? A sky? An alien from another planer? A disguised policeman? How did the rev trust him? Just like that?? An Iraqi Jew who will come and talk to the rabbi for hours and he will be in . . . ? They gave him a room in the attic. What is the meaning of this trust? The rabbi is smart, clever and wise! How did he attract the fear of her intelligent spiritual leader? Is it the charisma of Salman? She was thinking of ways to find out by self-answers to all these questions. Salman was like a seed of rice in a container of wheat and barley. He drew the attention of many. Many black hat people wanted his company. She can see from afar that he is engaged in long monologue while everyone is listening. What the hell is he telling them? Damn it! What is the story of this canary?

Fruma remembered that the rabbis of the past have said: Thinking about evil is worse than doing evil. Someone important said it. It is stupid she thought! She cursed and she felt embarrassed. Her mother thought her to spit after every bad word and say the shma and she will be forgiven. Fruma was amazed by all these laws, regulations, and customs, which were invented by man, and some people think that they are from an original divine source. People are funny, she thought. They invented stories and they begin to believe in them and finally they trap themselves in the fantasies of the stories and feel compelled to act them in their life.

Maybe Salman was a rich man who promised the rabbis tons of money in order to rebuild the old shul and to give money to many needy Jews in her group! Who knows? Salman is so close to her yet so far because she is a married woman and she cannot be near him or God forbid shake his hands. Her curiosity is growing like a new sapling that received a dose of water and some chemical nourishment. There is a way to milk new information. She will ask her husband clever and leading questions, tricking him to tell her more details about this new Elijah. She laughed at the comparison. After all, Elijah was also invisible. Ha! Ha! She giggled. No radio and no TV in their home/house. Only "shofar" the voice of the ultra orthodox community. Nothing really new in the above publication, she decided. Well! According to her husband Salman (he liked to be called in the Arabic version of shlemo)he was really from Kurdistan, North Iraq. He is a Kurd Jew. He was chuckling when he pronounced the word Kurd from some reason. She had already read that the basic theology of Sephardic Jews is "do little but do it right" as far as Halacha is concerned. Kurdistan sounded exotic but the reality was that the people are just people like all of us. Maybe?

Her husband has told her a familiar story with Jews. He heard that Salman came from a family of fourteen brothers and no sisters. His family in Kurdistan was a family of farmers who found ways to successfully grow tomatoes even in the cold weather of their region. They opened themselves a small factory of tomato juice, which was operated by the mother, the father and the brothers. The Madami family of Salman was originally from Persia. Salman has told Paltiel and told Fruma that it is possible that Kurdish Jews were the descendents of the ten lost tribes who arrived there in the eight century before the counting. The grave of the prophets Jonah and Nahum were in their area. After migration to Israel the Hadani, which was used to work hard in the mountainous soil of Kurdistan, has transferred their knowledge of tomatoes to the mountainous stubborn soil of Judea. Salman has become wealthy because he was able to hire cheap Arab laborers in his field and at the same time to send delicious tomatoes to the European market when harsh winters settled over Europe. He prospered; therefore, he built himself a huge villa in the middle of his agricultural settlement teasing those who lived in shacks and small apartments. Many of his brothers decided to build their own families. They begot children and he became known as Uncle Salman. Buckets of tomatoes were also his gifts to his nephews and nieces. Arab workers used to spread plastic carpet in his farm leaving the tomatoes to dry in the sunny days of the summer. The Madani sauce was on the table of almost every Israeli who liked pasta. Salman always smiled when he was asked about the secretive ingredients of his tomato sauce. It is from

God he used to tease any noisy man of the trade. Paltiel told her that he was invited to Salman's room to eat one day and the tomato salad that he tasted there had the taste of the Garden of Eden. So unique, so tasty, so delicious. Paltiel promised not to leave him alone before he tells him the hidden secrets of his tomato salad.

Fruma was just listening attentively to the stories about Salman, the tomato man from the bus on wheels. Paltiel revealed that Salman is quite sharp when it comes to business and money and maybe just maybe the rabbi can learn from him about beneficial investments. Paltiel was taken by Salman the Kurdi and he felt like he knew him for years. Salman lost it all in a large, unsuccessful investment in addition to the fire that consumed his factory and villa. In New York he tried to begin his business again, but in these economic times he was without any success. He tried being a bus boy to survive and he felt humiliated. He sang the routine Israeli songs in pretentious Bar and Bat Mitzvahs, but these jobs could not pay the rent. Many months passed without any connections to his large family. He was always alone, come to think about it. Never married. Very unusual in the traditional Kurdish world. He also said being a bachelor is like being an independent Turkish sultan and he wasn't to keep it this way. They suspected that he was homosexual, he told Paltiel, but he swore to God that he loves woman, but from afar. Paltiel described Salman as a handsome guy with penetrating eyes that can either kill a person or love him to death. Paltiel knew that Salman came to them because he became homeless. All visions and dreams about help from the rich have collapsed and squeezed like ripened tomatoes. However, Paltiel added: The guy wanted to return to Hashem and his holy torah. No Jew should be prevented from repenting, praying and offering "tzedaka." In addition, he is trying to convince the rabbi to purchase land in a near by farm and to grow tomatoes. He spoke in details about his success in Kurdistan and Israel and he promised to enrich the congregation in this investment. The rabbi was quite skeptical, but he listened. Salman was a smart Jew, declared Paltiel. He began to study Talmud days and nights. His knowledge of Hebrew and Aramaic is impressive and his mind is so legalistic, like a fine businessman. He found God suddenly. He lost him after he left Iraq. There God was so personal that it was a pleasure to meet him. In Israel he was told by the securalist/Zionist/Socialist Jews that God is not on their agenda. He is only on the agenda of Jews who are not evolved . . .

Fruma listened and absorbed every word of Paltiel about Salman. She pretended not to be especially interested in this tale, but her hidden look could only confirm many points of her husband's narration concerning Salman. We are all uprooted, even in our place of birth, thought Fruma. We are a unit by ourselves and we create this coziness with our friends and family, but deeply in the depth of our depths we are lonely and alone. She did not want to dwell on this thought because she can become very depressed about the meaning that all of us couldn't find. Fruma thought that was God's plan for men and women. To search and search and search with no results. He put us to wander in the vast Sinai desert just to kill us. No one saw the Promised Land. What is the meaning of walking forty years in order to die there? All of a sudden Salman's story began to make no sense. It is a human's destiny to investigate any meaning and end with hope to find it. The investment in this search can exhaust any person. What kind of God is this Hasidic God? He went into a coma? Unaware of her confusion, delusion, disappointment and fear? Did he care if she is woman and not a man?

Paltiel took a moment to relax from his intensive recitation of Salman's journey. Without warning he added, "Why am I telling you all this, Fruma?" Fruma shrugged her shoulder and she continued to sort and fold the laundry in their routine order. There is something about Salman that has created unsettling emotions. The only thought that she can think about now is to squeeze more tomatoes and eat them like a hungry cat that would push his sharp nail into the red fruit. She was wondering if the forbidden fruit was tomato after all. The holy Torah, in her typical way, leaves many things for the imagination.

# Chapter 4

Fruma, like a nightingale bird who can sing but no one is there to hear her beautiful songs, was fearful of the changes of her mind. She was wondering how we all start somewhere and often finishes nowhere. She would love to hear the story directly from Salman without a narrator called husband. She really, really loved him, her husband. She got used to him. He is basically a decent and caring man, but the girls were born and they are the joy of her life, but Paltiel is something else. He is not her romantic life at all. He loved to use biblical expressions and praise her, but it is always in dedication to her children and to the cleanliness of the house. "I love you." "I desire you." "You attract me" is not in his grammar and syntax. It would be nice if he would compliment her about her natural intelligence, curiosity and cleverness, but not a syllable in this department. She convinced herself when she was a teenager that God blessed her with Paltiel. Pious, and a man of the holy book. Never missed an opportunity to give the needy from their meager income. Like her sewing, her life was being connected through loose strings, which have become one solid dress. It seems to her now that it will be impossible to disintegrate the entire sweater into its original particles. She was only one particle of common fabric, but now she is surrounded by so many ties, connections and unseen fabrications lying down in the final product. She loves working in their garden harvesting her tomatoes in a tiny military routine, unaccepted by the dynamics of life. She needs to let her brain absorb new material besides the religious stuff. She is saturated by all these endless rituals and prayers, supplications, and blessings. No time of rest. Just to have more dialogue with herself. Is it a conspiracy to keep the believer constantly busy in order to have time to independently think for him or herself? Questions are delayed and establishing safe indicators to receive religious responses have begun to stifle her creativity. She is smart enough to know that secularists have similar dilemmas with only one difference: God has left them and they left God and they try to find answers in other human beings. In the haredi community women are supposed to be heard a little and be rarely seen and be by themselves.

Like every accidental event Salman was shopping with tomatoes in the market of Jews with black yarmulkes. The aroma of Friday morning market was in the air. Fish, chicken and men with bloody aprons, called butchers. Vegetables, fruit, lox and bagels, cream cheese and a million varieties of the soul. All with the seal of the religious High Court of the Haredim. This higher authority under the God indivisible meant everything to these shoppers. How can someone celebrate shabbes without gefiltefish? All kinds. Salty, semi-salty and quarter salty. Just pay and you buy these plum, juicy tomatoes, well placed in carton boxes ready to be desired, eaten and consumed by those who need to pursue his wet love of the lips, the mouth and beyond. He was walking with a stick! Erect, with busy black beard. Hasidic uniform and a hat larger than his skull. Brown like the mud men, the Euphrates and the Tigris. Brown deep eyes of a wandering Bedouin. A nose like the beak of an eagle, but handsome and impressive, which forces you to look at him. He was murmuring words of prayer in a Sephardic Hebrew accent. So this is the way of the Iraqi Jew, look? He looked like an Hispanic soldier not far, far from their home. He was chatting with everyone in the market as if he knew everyone for years. She caught from afar his smile with his bright teeth. In a second of human encounter his eyes and Fruma's eyes experienced a silent encounter that only men and women can interpret. Fear, desire, familiarity, and longing were concentrated in this split second. His reddish tomatoes were placed in a bag made out of plastic, but her tomatoes were scattered all over the huge brown bag. He turned to see her running as fast as she can in the opposite direction. As if she encountered the devil himself. He saw her back in her galloping step toward the edge of the Friday market. He was mesmerized, like her. Her look was mysterious, communicative and familiar. The shock of this brief encounter left him baffled. He knew this look, but he could not locate its time and place.

Paltiel was charmed by Salman stories about the wonders of Babylonia-Iraq. Salman knew the art of tales and legends, with flowery translated syntax from Hebrew and Arabic. He brought their shtetel Jews a breath of nostalgic emotion which was usually suppressed in order to create a communal order. He was emotional with a ringing voice and he never restrained himself from showing his inner feelings. Very unusual in a society demanding low key in emotional expressions. Paltiel even related a story about Salman's beautiful voice. Totally different from their Hasidic ululation and crying inclinations. His songs were like the beats of the drum, like the vibrations of the flute. Quarter tones with thousands of improvisations. "Like the beat of the heart," said Paltiel about Salman's songs, "no beat is equal to other beats when it comes to the heart." Fruma is being pulled by these magnetic feelings of the visible encounter and was both delighted and scared when Palti decided to invite Salman to be their guest for Shabbat dinner. All daughters sat on one side of the table after they helped their mother all afternoon in the art of cooking, which was very unusual. Palti explained to his family the commandment of hospitality in Judaism and asked everyone to be polite and well behaved. Salman did not say much this evening. He was just honored to be blessed over the wine with his ringing Arabic melody. Amazed, curious and fascinated by this exotic Jew, Fruma only ran back and forth to the kitchen making all efforts to ignore his look. She felt his eyes on her back. He felt her look by her presence, observing her delicate catwalk. Palti is involved in his food consuming process, unaware of the human electricity in the room. Her daughters were oblivious to anything but their expectation to retire to their rooms. After the gastronomic stage, songs praising God and blessing over the food just followed like a surrealistic, slow, black and white movie. In his way out he said good shabbes, walking like Jacob after he was struck on his thigh by his ankle. From her kitchen she heard sporadic talk between Palteil and Salman. Paltiel was trying to find him a pious woman from the congregation and Salman insisted that he is so busy learning, studying, and loving Hashem that no time is left for a woman. Palti was not giving up. He asked him to keep it in mind because he has an excellent female candidate in mind. It is customary to leave the guest with baskets of food to retrieve and to be taken home with him. Fruma packed up many delicate cooked food and placed a nice ripe tomato at the top of a huge lot full of fruit and vegetables. Salman just nodded his head with thumbs and a wide smile has covered his entire face. Fruma blushed and returned to her bedroom.

This is the first night in which she refused Palti's advances. She began sobbing with uncontrolled tears. Palti just accepted her exhausted headache syndrome and went to sleep snoring like an old locomotive trying to climb up a high hill. Salman went to his room walking in the dark. Only tiny night bulbs were shining his shadows to his bed. At the end of the Sabbath he sat down and in eloquent Hebrew verses he wrote: "Only when someone found hell and lived through it he will never have to return to the Far end of Eden", and he added "like a crow and a dove we have to live on different branches of a tree, not able to fly to each other." Salman was shrewd like a Byzantine prince. The old lady who helped Fruma clean the house before the holiday has sworn to deliver the note to Fruma. With the utmost secret fashion, he told her that he is sending a special blessing for one of Fruma's daughters who could not sleep at night. He convinced her that the prayer is an old kabalistic prayer from a holy Iraqi Jew. Fruma was stunned and confused. She read it again and again until she burned it slowly in order to see traces to their final life.

The old lady, innocent in her deliverance, has become the postmaster of words about experience, pain, attraction and forbidden fruits of words. She wrote once: "I am like a bird fearing my cage and freedom at the same time. But you are like a wild eagle that can fly anytime you want.

You are pursuing too close to the circles to protect your sanity and I am encircled by womanhood and a God who constantly fought each other." At the wedding of the chief reb's daughter, Hasidic men sweating and dancing back to back with praises to Elohim in heaven, declaring the mysterious power of their Shepherd. Reciting poetic praises to the young bride and groom who fear God like Ruth and Esther. Etc. Etc. Etc. The same old song and dance, women with other women. Singing in their groups, gossiping about dowries and virginity and praising the God who constantly talks about himself to discriminate against them. Instead of rice and candies, a mysterious yeshiva student began pelting his friends with tomatoes and the frenzy just only began. They were giggling like hell while they're playing "got you!" with the red pluming fruit. All was done in a good spirit and the reb even laughed at the scene of tomato—men and women enjoying and implicating gentle hits on each other. She was able to see him and spot him in a sea of a hundred black hats. Salman was hugging men and kissing them with the excitement of a devoted Nazarene and in a sincere fashion. This time he hesitantly lifted his hand in the air to map his place in the ocean of men and to signal his communication with Fruma in the midst of her semi-hysterical female friends.

# Chapter 5

The Jewish guilt was unbearable. She is longing for something or someone where other haredi are quite happy with their lot. She cannot discuss this with anyone, even with the old lady messenger who innocently was transferring all these general and generalistic messages. She thought one day to leave it all behind her. Just like all of us she wished just to disappear and break the past into pieces. Dreams about Salman have caused her to get up swearing and frightened. She needed her good Palti to comfort her. "Dreams are false reality," he used to quote Solomon, the wise king of Israel. Salman was incredible in her dreams. He made her a real woman. His kisses were warm, Semitic and juicy. He kissed her in places in which Palti would not dare to touch. Her nipples were so aroused that the color of tomatoes took over their usual brown color. Her private part was also the color of his intensive engagement. Gasping, breathing heavily. And the greatest of all illusions was his whispering in her ear his words of love, which included total dedication to her body, soul and the uncompromising statement about his need for her. She was convinced that even imagined sexual relations with a stranger is a sin, but little by little she began to enjoy the scenery, but always feeling down after she got up. She found many excuses to shop everyday. Fresh fruit and vegetables, she said to Palti, are healthy. In addition, she was breaking boredom. Salman was about a short distance from her bargaining articulations about chickens. She was wonderful in this area. Salman was squeezing cucumbers and tomatoes as usual. Also bargaining but with an oriental flavor. Like an Iranian man of trade. Always gentle in his approach. She could not hear the words, but she could easily sense his movements of his hands and his legs. Those eyes again struck her like a tone of merchandise. He is clearly telling her that his desire is imminent and his wish to physically embrace her is obvious. All in this his Arab penetrating eyes. She returned her look to him. This time he placed his middle finger on his lips and kissed them with such devotion than one can see only when a religious Jew kisses his Torah. He went one forward the coming week. In the air he wrote in Hebrew: "I knew you from before." She dared to write in the air: "I always knew you." It was possible to split the air through electric humanity and they returned to their nests. Unable to wait until the next existing moments. Like the candles of Hanukkah they are allowed to watch them but to make no personal use of them. This is the Jewish law. She began to send him notes with the elderly woman from her cooking. Paltiel only praised her for the mitzvah that she just fulfilled: caring for the stranger, the lonely and any Jew from any place. With attention to detail, she cooked for him all these spicy foods with rice, tomatoes and zucchini. He always returned the dishes clean and sparkling.

And then one day, without warning, she found a tiny paper inside one of the sealed dishes telling her that he cannot remove her image from his mind and that women came and went in his life but all that he wishes is to encounter her looks in the flea market. This was too much. Fruma knew that men know how to drop attractive words but they select them carefully because their commitment is also shaky and unstable. She wrote that no one will die from looking and she is eager to see him again from a distance. She was afraid that her emotions are taking her to a path of seduction and attraction, but her inner forces compelled her gently to remove the handkerchief from her head for a split second, revealing her beautiful reddish hair to his curious looks. She must speak to the rabitizen about these tortures of the heart, but the wife of the reb was an expert in spreading intimate secrets of women among other women. She was contemplating telling Paltiel, but she is aware that her life is like a one-way street. No highways and no-byways. She got stuck, like a fly in a jar of honey. She knew that she was caught like a gambler, losing it all or receiving a noticeable price. So much to gain and so much to lose at the same time. All her prayers reached their limits. All supplications ended in vain. She was left with her soul in the dialogue of the deaf. Only echoes were heard in her ringing conscious. Salman is only a legend, she rationalized. I really did not even know him. He never spoke to me, but God has placed him in my mind and soul: unable to reach and unable to run away. Months passed and, like an anchorwoman, she was left hanging between the surface of the water and the depth of the sea. Like "teko" in the Talmud. God likes this game. Who is she to overcome the mighty hero of heaven and earth? She doubts his compassion, but few fear. What he installed in her never left her. Salman just vanished suddenly. Paltiel only said, "God gives and God takes, may his name be blessed." Only green tomatoes remain hanging on her sukkah.

AKIBA HEBREW ACADEMY

BVG